CW01640783

Our mission is to provide readers with a pocket-sized read in the places where they are waiting, relaxing, taking a break. We aim to support writers by giving them a new market for their short stories and short non-fiction.

Don't forget to visit our website www.leafbooks.co.uk to tell us what you think of this book and to learn more about the writer and our other services.

Enjoy!

First published by Leaf Books Ltd in 2006


Leaf Books are proud to be working with the
University of Glamorgan

www.leafbooks.co.uk

Leaf
GTi Suite,
Valleys Innovation Centre,
Navigation Park,
Abercynon,
CF45 4SN

Printed by Allprint
www.allprint.ltd.uk

ISBN 1-905599-07-2
ISBN 978-1-905599-07-3

# The Rehearsal

by

Douglas Bruton

Leaf 3

Douglas Bruton is a teacher of English at a Scottish High School and lives in a small village just outside Edinburgh. A fledgling member of The Pentland Writers' Group, his story 'An Angel Passed Through' won the Slingink International Prize for Short Fiction 2005 and 'The Book of Possible Loves' was the overall winner in the Wellington Town Council short story competition 2005.

# The Rehearsal

He closed the front door, shutting out the work-a-day world. He dropped a worn brown leather briefcase in the hall, slipped free of his suit jacket, tore loose the knot of his tie and shed his workday skin. The briefcase fell with a heavy thump, like an emphatic conclusion, like a final full stop, bringing to an end the long day he had spent thumbing paper behind a paper-strewn desk.

He carried a crisp new carrier bag weighed down with shopping through to the kitchen and let its contents spill out onto the work surface. He sorted and resorted the items, arranging them with all the ceremony and reverence of a priest preparing to intone mass. He shuffled them into groupings, then rearranged them, organising and reorganising them as he had earlier organised the paper on his desk.

He checked the clock on the wall against his watch and nodded approval of their synchronicity. He was on schedule. Tonight would run like clockwork. He had planned it over and over in his head, rehearsed each detail again and again.

In the living room, he paused briefly before pulling the curtains closed; paused just long enough to register the dimly lit empty streets below and the blank brickwork and the blind windows opposite. Then he shut out the ordinary world.

He knelt in front of a new stacked hi-fi system – the CD player, the amplifier, the tape machine and the tuner sitting one on top of the other like the in-trays and out-trays on his desk, only here they were neatly and precisely positioned and free from dusty and dog-eared documents. He flipped the switch on the CD player and waited. The machine shunted and clicked, found and then read the CD he'd left in the drawer ready for this night. The word ‘play’ flashed on the display screen, the three bars of the graphic equaliser jerked rhythmically in front of him and suddenly soft music was released into the air. He adjusted the volume, increased it slightly; stopped to listen and then turned it back to the original setting.

He adjusted the lighting too, up a notch and then down again until he was satisfied that it was just as he had planned. He cast a critical eye over the dining table tucked away in one corner of the room. It was set for two: two matching place mats with carefully placed arrangements of knives, forks and spoons, and two neatly folded and pleated napkins clasped in two identical silver rings. He had bought the cutlery specially. The handles were heavy and scrolled with an ornate swirling pattern, like bindweed coiled around the smooth stem of a young plant. They were part of a set: six soup spoons, six dessert spoons, six teaspoons, six small forks, six large forks, six of everything. He'd contemplated inviting others tonight, a real dinner party. He even made a list. But in the end the thought of conducting so much conversation, when all he really wanted was to talk to her – to listen to her talk – put him off the idea. Two crystal glasses and the two gilt candlesticks placed either side of a floral centrepiece created some height as well as establishing a balanced symmetry. One of the new candles had slipped free of its true vertical. He lifted the holder, straightened the red wax finger and replaced it carefully – aligning it with all the precision and attention to detail of a mathematician.

He retreated without taking his eyes off the table, like an artist surveying a painting he had just put the finishing brushstrokes to. 'A work in progress,' he said out loud. He wondered if it was too much. An overblown cliché, or an overdressed stage set? He wondered what she would think and decided it was a bit overdone. He removed the floral centrepiece – an arrangement of assorted white and yellow lilies festooned with gossamer sprays of white gypsophilia. He placed it on the mantelpiece. He also removed one of the candlesticks and hid it behind a pile of books. He stood back to reassess the work. 'Better,' he pronounced, and satisfied that it was all just right, he left the room.

In the kitchen he rolled up his shirtsleeves and began preparing the meal. He had seen the whole thing spread across two pages of a supermarket magazine. The photographs made each stage of the meal seem like a separate work of art – not a succession of flat paintings, but a series of constructions, a display of spectacular edible sculptures. The meal was designed to impress. It was another perfect piece in his elaborate jigsaw. He had begun by poring over the recipes, assessing his competence to carry out each line of the step-by-step instructions. Then he practised each stage until he mastered the different skills and was familiar with each part of the process. He had compiled lists and drawn up colour-coded 'time maps' for the execution of each dish. Finally, he rehearsed the procedure again and again until the cooking of the meal was itself something of a well-oiled performance.

He checked the heat under a bubbling pot; checked the progress against his written instructions; checked his watch against the kitchen clock again. He was not surprised to find that everything was going according to plan.

He felt lighter, walked taller, already the hero of his own imagination. He whistled along with the music as he retraced his steps to the front door, collecting his discarded clothes on the way. She would come tonight and he would be ready. It was time. He had watched her from afar for long enough.

He folded his suit trousers over a wooden hanger, draped his suit jacket over the top and filed the hanger away in the walk-in cupboard in his bedroom. He bundled the rest of the clothes he'd worn that day into the laundry basket. He stood naked before the bed and inspected the clothes he had laid out that morning. They were still on their hangers and he had arranged them so that a flattened version of himself was there on the clean-sheeted bed. He nodded his approval again, fussed over the collar of the shirt till it sat sharply pointed and brushed invisible lint off one leg of the trousers.

Nothing had been left to chance. This night was to be special.

He passed through to the bathroom and turned on the shower. The water spat and hissed fitfully. He let the jets play through his fingers, waiting for the temperature to settle and the water to run even and hot. He removed his watch, noting the time as he placed it face up next to the sink. He counted the minutes left before she would be there. He briefly examined his reflection in the mirror and then stepped into the cubicle and pulled the door shut behind him. He braced himself against the tiled wall, his head bent forward and the water stinging the arch of his back. He looked at his feet and watched the silver strings of water slide from his body and snake away down the drain.

He jerked himself free from the wall, his eyes closed and his face raised to meet the full force of the shower. He ran his hands over his face and through his hair and snorted loudly. He thought of her. He bent his head again and spat at the floor. He reached for the soap without looking and rubbed under each arm until a thick lather formed. The suds dripped from him and gathered in a foamy puddle that hid his toes for a moment. He lifted his head again and ran the bar of soap down his chest and across his abdomen.

The astringent smell of lemons filled the cubicle. He wondered what she smelled of. He'd stood behind her in a queue once. He remembered studying her hair, the way the light played over the surface, the way the different colours sat against each other. He always thought she had straight black hair that fell to her shoulders like a hood of silk cloth. Up close he could see the infinite variations in colour: the dark blueish hues, the gradations of charcoal black and the darkest browns. He had been close enough to pick out the individual strands. There were threads of silver there too. He had tried to edge closer, hoping to get near enough to breathe in her perfume without anyone noticing. The queue had lurched forward suddenly and the opportunity had passed.

He chased the lather down through his groin and over his thighs. He raised one leg at a time, balancing like a wading bird on the other, as he massaged the soap between his toes and over the sole of each foot. He left his hair till last, squirting a generous gobbet of blue shampoo straight onto his head. He waited until he felt the coolness of the liquid seep through the hair to his scalp, then he scrubbed his stiffened fingers in a circular motion over the dome of his head until he was sporting a crooked crown of soapy bubbles. The shampoo smelled of coconut, a sweet, almost sickly smell that conflicted with the pungent lemon scent of the soap. He didn't notice.

He stuck his head out of the cubicle to check the time. He felt that he had lingered too long. The bathroom mirror was steamed over and rivulets of condensation ran in slow motion tears down the glass. The face of his watch was also hidden behind a smudge of steam. He dipped back into the shower and hurriedly rinsed off the rest of the soap.

After hastily checking on the food simmering away in the kitchen, he retreated to the bedroom where he inexpertly dried himself off. He ignored the cooling dampness at the small of his back. He was a little behind time now. He dragged a brush through his hair, sprayed on too much body spray, and rushed back to the kitchen without dressing. He smiled to himself at the thought that she might arrive early.

He consulted his cooking instructions and set about preparing the vegetables. He threw them in the sink and flicked the cold tap on. The fierce rush of water thundered against the steel surface and splashed over the edge of the sink and over his stomach. He leapt back as if stung. He cursed out loud and scrambled to turn the water off. The clock told him he was only four minutes behind. He took a breath and adopted a more careful pace. No need to panic, he muttered. He scrubbed the vegetables clean and arranged them in neat rows on the chopping board. He selected a knife from the knife-block and began the practiced dissection of carrots and parsnips.

The timer on the oven buzzed like an angry fly in flight. The knife slipped from his hand and clattered on the wooden cutting board. No need to panic, he repeated, steadying himself. He reset the timer and opened the oven door. A gasp of hot air escaped and he checked his movement for a moment. Then he crouched down to inspect the meat.

Back in the bedroom he wiped his watch dry and slipped it back over his wrist. Then he dressed in front of a full-length mirror, returning each empty hanger to the walk-in wardrobe. Not long now. He applied two short squirts of aftershave to his neck and made his way into the living room.

He opened a drawer and rummaged amongst

the concealed disorder until he found a half spent book of matches. He tore one match from the book and pulled it roughly across the strip of strike paper. It hissed into flame. Holding the strip of card between finger and thumb, he leaned across the table and lit the lone candle.

From the fridge he collected a chilled bottle of white wine. He didn't know if she liked her wine sweet or dry. Indeed, he didn't know if she preferred red to white. He'd chosen a medium white. He hoped it was alright. He peeled away the foil from the neck of the bottle and twisted an old–fashioned corkscrew into the plastic cork. He put the bottle between his knees and pulled the cork free with a forced pop.

He poured himself a glass of wine. He was ready. He replaced the bottle in the door of the fridge. Everything was ready. He looked at his watch and checked it against the kitchen clock yet again. It was time. He returned to the stacked hi-fi and set the CD back to track one. He watched the three bars of the graphic equaliser restart their restless gyrations. She could come now.

He felt the minutes creep in and out again. He sipped at the wine, noticing its coolness on his lips. It had a funny taste. He preferred his wine dry. He tasted it again and decided it was probably fine. He held the glass by the stem and lifted it to the light as he had seen them do on a recent wine programme. He twisted the stem in his fingers, letting the wine roll around the inside of the glass.

'A buttery colour,' he pronounced, pretending some expertise.

Track one faded and track two began. She was late. It was allowed. It was expected. He wondered how late was acceptable. He flipped the CD to the start of track one once more.

He parted the curtains for a moment and looked down on the street. A car pulled away – a taxi cab, its lights cutting a path through the darkness. It was her, he convinced himself. It had to be. He closed the curtains and went to open the front door. He didn't care if it seemed a little too eager. Somewhere he thought he heard the heavy thump of the lift doors closing and the muffled screech of the winding mechanism.

She was not too late. He checked his watch. It seemed acceptable.

'Sorry! Hope I'm not late,' she said.

'No, not at all. It's fine,' he said, standing back to let her in. He took her coat and hung it on a hanger that in turn hung on a hook on the back of the door.

'Thanks.' She smiled nervously and fiddled with the thin strap of a small black leather handbag. She was wearing a black dress flecked with silver with matching low-heeled shoes. He had seen the dress displayed on an awkwardly posed mannequin in a store window the week before. He'd thought of her when he had seen it. It did not look awkward on her. He had known it wouldn't. He thought of telling her this, but decided against it.

'Come in,' he said instead, and gestured theatrically towards the living room.

He followed her through, close enough to see again the silver in her hair.

'Can I get you a drink, Melissa?' He felt uncertain of using her name, though he had rehearsed this line again and again. Melissa, Melissa, Melissa. He thought she smiled, liking the sound of her name on his lips. 'Maybe a glass of wine?'

'I'd love a glass of white wine, thanks.'

'Perfect, make yourself at home. I'll just be a tick.' He hurried away to the kitchen.

'Something smells good,' Melissa called through to him.

'Yeah, I hope you like it.' He inspected the glass and gave it a final polish before pouring in the wine.

'Can I help at all?'

He knew she would say that – that she would offer. He liked that she did.

'No, no. It's okay.' He checked his list of instructions, turned down the heat under the vegetables and returned to the living room. 'All under control,' he said, placing her wine on the low table in front of her. 'All under control,' he repeated, smiling confidently.

'Thanks,' she said.

'Cheers.' He half-raised his own half-empty glass to her.

'This is really sweet.'

He thought she meant the wine.

'All of this.' She indicated the table set for two. 'You've gone to some trouble. The candle and everything.'

'Hope I haven't overdone it. Just thought your first visit here should be special.'

He caught the flashed smile she sent him. He

wondered if she had read in that word 'first' that there would be other nights like this.

'I like it. It does make it special. It's nice.'

Nice, he thought.

She ran the back of one finger down her cheek, catching a miscreant curl of hair and tucking it behind her ear. It was a habit he had watched replayed time after time over her work. He took another mouthful of wine, unsure of how to proceed.

'It's a nice flat,' she said.

'Yeah, it is. I'll give you a tour, if you like.' He placed his almost empty glass next to her full one.

'A tour?'

'Of the flat.'

'Oh, okay.'

He wanted to reach for her hand, but thought it too soon. There was no rush. He had the whole evening. 'Mind you, a tour makes it sound like something grand. It's not much...

but it's home.' He instantly regretted the line. It was something his mother would have said.

'It feels like a home,' said Melissa. 'Warm and welcoming.'

'Well, this is the living room.' He pirouetted on one foot with one outstretched arm to indicate the room they were in. 'And dining area,' he added, pointing to the table.

She smiled and nodded.

'And through here is the kitchen.' He led the way.

Melissa followed. 'Signs of activity in here,' she said, pretending not to look at the open pages of the supermarket magazine. He snatched up the bottle of wine and moved on without stopping.

'And the hall, you've seen,' he said presenting it to her again.

'The bathroom.' He opened the door briefly. The towels hung tidily over the edge of the bath and the condensation on the mirror had cleared.

'And...the bedroom.' He tried not to place any special emphasis on this last room. He didn't want her to think that he expected anything of her. He retrieved a stray discarded sock from the middle of the floor and dropped it in the laundry basket. 'Sorry.'

'Yes, it feels like a home,' she giggled.

He had seen her giggling at her desk once. She'd been on the phone. He'd thought then that it had a pleasant sound – like running water. And here she was giggling in his bedroom, just for him.

'And that's it.'

'It's so tidy.'

'Sorry,' he said, feeling almost guilty.

'No, it's nice.' That word again – 'nice'. He wondered if she really meant it.

'It's so unexpected,' she added.

That was a better word, he thought, a real word.

'Yes, that's it, unexpected.'

'For someone with such an untidy desk, you mean?' he joked.

'Well, yes.' She laughed. They both laughed. They were back in the living room. He sat beside her this time, his leg almost touching hers. He noted her glass was still full and refilled his own. He counted the seconds of silence, searching for something to say.

'I didn't think you'd come,' he ventured at last.

'Was I so late?' she said.

'No, not tonight. When I asked you. I didn't think you'd want to.'

'Why not?'

'I don't know. I just...' She brushed a hand against his arm. It was the lightest of touches, so fleeting he might have imagined it.

'I was waiting to be asked,' she said.

He felt her leg against his now, thought he felt her warmth on his thigh. He had wanted to ask her for so long. He wanted to confess that to her now, to tell her of the weeks he had spent watching her from behind his wall of paper, waiting for the 'right moment' and never noticing the passing of so many right moments. He wanted to tell her how real this all felt.

Suddenly the timer in the kitchen began buzzing again.

'I'm just glad you're here now,' he said.

'Me too.'

There was a pause. It felt almost awkward. He wondered if this was one of those moments, one of those 'right moments' that called for some action. It felt like something out of a book. She looked into his eyes, he into hers. They leaned towards each other. He felt her breath on him, warm and fresh with a taste of mint.

'Shouldn't you get that?'

'What?' he said.

‘Wouldn’t want to spoil the meal when you have gone to so much trouble.’

He became aware of the sound of the timer coming from the kitchen. The moment receded.

‘No, you’re right.’ He leapt to his feet and disappeared into the kitchen again.

‘This looks too good to eat,’ she said when they sat down to the first course.

He topped up his wine glass.

‘I didn’t know you could cook.’

‘Anyonc can cook. You just have to practise.’

‘But this is so...’ Melissa was lost for words.

‘Lots of practice.’ Despite his show of false modesty, he couldn’t really hide how pleased he was that it had turned out right. It was just like the picture in the magazine.

‘Everything is so...’ again Melissa ran out

of words.

The candle flickered, its dancing light caught and copied in so many surfaces so that the whole table seemed to sparkle. It was like something from a dream, he thought.

'You'll have to teach me,' said Melissa.

'It's easy.'

He left her alone whilst he was busy with preparations for the second course. He was aware that she was very quiet. He imagined her examining the detail of his room in an effort to know him better. He thought of her running her fingers along the books lined to perfect attention on his bookshelves, noting his reading habits, perhaps being impressed with the breadth of his taste. He pictured her taking a particular volume down and leafing through its unsullied pages, though he couldn't decide which book she would select. Perhaps she studied the paintings hung on his walls or the carefully arranged clutter. He hoped it all said the right thing. He hoped she liked it all.

'You okay?' he called through, keeping her in his thoughts and fearing, suddenly, that she might have evaporated into the air.

'You've read all these?' she asked.

'What?' He marched ceremoniously into the room carrying aloft his second construction in food.

'These books, have you read them all?'

'Most of them.'

'They're all fiction,' she observed.

'I like to escape. Don't you? Fiction is my way of escaping.'

'But so many books! I don't know where you get the time.'

'It's all I do.'

'Apart from cooking,' she said, marvelling at the plate he had set before her.

'I suppose that's an escape too when I am cooking for you, Melissa.' He'd said her name again. It felt more natural this time. Her eyes flashed across the table at him. It was another one of those moments, he thought. He wondered how many of them he could fit into a single evening with Melissa.

'You say the nicest things,' she said, sending him another of her smiles, smiles he had only seen gifted to others in the office until now.

The food tasted expensive, like something ordered from some splendid restaurant. He was pleased with himself and, creating a gap in the conversation, he began composing a food review in his head full of flattering ingredients. Then he decided that this was not the time and deleted the thought.

'What do you do to escape?' he asked her. He didn't really know anything about her – only what he had seen in the office and what he had made up in imagining a night with her. 'You know, for fun; to forget work. What do you do?'

Suddenly, before she could answer, the

phone began ringing. Everything stopped. The whole charade collapsed like a house of cards. The ringing went on and on, insistent and shrill, demanding 'answer me, answer me!' He cursed under his breath; he'd forgotten to switch it off at the wall. The illusion was broken. He sat like an actor who has forgotten his lines and waited for the ringing to stop.

When it did, it stopped as suddenly as it had started, leaving behind a silence that was even more audible. He looked at the empty seat opposite, where only a moment before Melissa had sat smiling across at him. He stared at her unsipped glass of wine; he saw her food untouched and congealing on the plate. He waited, hoping that the night could pick up where it had left off, but knowing in his heart that the curtain had fallen on this performance.

He pushed back his chair and got up from the table. His crumpled napkin unfurled, slid from his lap and fell to the floor like the ceremonial lowering of a flag. He didn't notice. He found the phone, yanked the cord from the wall, picked up the receiver and held it to his ear.

'Hello, Melissa? No, it's no trouble. Really. I never really expected... No, I understand. Completely. Another time perhaps. Yes, fine. See you then.'

He hung up the phone.

'Another time,' he sighed to himself. He returned to his seat at the table. He cupped one hand around the flame of the lone candle, leaned forward and blew it out.

'Next week,' he said.